W9-ASI-679
DEC 1981
RECEIVED
OHIO DOMINICAN
COLLEGE LIBRARY
COLUMBUS, OHIO
43219

by JANET SCHULMAN
pictures by MARYLIN HAFNER

GREENWILLOW BOOKS
A Division of William Morrow & Company, Inc., New York

 Inquiries should be addressed to Greenwillow Books, 105 Madison Avenue, New York, N.Y. 10016.
Printed in the United States of America. First Edition 1 2 3 4 5 6 7 8 9 10



Library of Congress Cataloging in Publication Data
Schulman, Janet. Camp KeeWee's secret weapon. (Greenwillow read-alone)
Summary: Jill's softball talent helps her to find her niche at camp.
[1. Camping–Fiction 2. Softball–Fiction] I. Hafner, Marylin.
II. Title. PZ7.S3866Cam [E] 78-16742
ISBN 0-688-80185-4 ISBN 0-688-84185-6 lib. bdg.

FOR CAITY AND HER PAL NIKKI

–J. S.

FOR AVA, SUSAN, AND ADA,
WINNERS ALL

–M.H.

# Contents

# Girls Can't Play

School was out
and there was nothing to do.
Jill's best friend, Polly,
was at camp.
Her second best friend
was at her grandmother's.

Even the girl next door,
who would only play house,
was away for the summer.
Maybe there are some kids
at the playground, Jill thought.

She was right.
There were lots of kids
at the playground:

kids with pull toys,

kids in the sandbox,

kids on tricycles.
"Nothing but babies here,"
said Jill.

She walked to the ball field.
Some boys were playing softball.
Two of them were in Jill's class.
"Hi, David! Hi, Jim!"
she called.
They nodded to her
and kept right on playing.

Jill's favorite game was softball.
But she almost never
got a chance to play it.
They didn't play softball
in her school gym class.

And the boys wouldn't let her
play with them after school.

Jill stood behind the fence
and watched the boys play.
Suddenly one of them
looked at his watch.
"I'm late for the dentist,"
he shouted.
And he ran off the field.
"Oh, no!" groaned his team.

The game was tied 5-5.
Now the other team
had an extra player.
It wasn't fair.

Then David whispered to Jim.
Jim nodded and said something
to the other boys.

They all turned
and looked at Jill.
"Hey, do you want to play?"
David called to Jill.
"Sure!" she said.
"You can play right field.
You won't have to do much,"
he said.
But he was wrong.
The first batter up
hit a high fly ball
to right field.

Jill watched the ball
and got ready to catch it.
"I'll get it!" yelled a big boy.
He ran toward Jill.
Crash! He ran right into Jill.
They both fell down.

But the ball was
already in Jill's hand.
And she held on to it.

All the boys on Jill's team cheered.
All but the big boy.
He looked embarrassed.

## Change of Plans

Jill went home happy.
Her team had won.
And the boys had said
she could play with them again.
"Boy, I am going to have
a great summer!" she said
to her mother and father.

“And how!” said her father.

“You are going to go to camp!”

Jill’s mouth fell open.

“But you said we

couldn’t afford camp,” she said.

"We can now," said her father.
"Your mother got a job today."
Her mother looked happy.
So did her father.
But Jill did not.
"All the camps started
two weeks ago," said Jill.
"We found one that has agreed
to let you start late.
It's Camp KeeWee,"
said her father.

"Is Polly there?" asked Jill.
"No, but you'll make friends,"
said her mother.

"You can go boating
and swimming
and horseback riding,"
said her father.
"But I don't want to go boating
and swimming
and horseback riding.
I want to play softball
with the boys," said Jill.
"Oh, dear." Her mother sighed.

Then her father said,
"Well, I'm sorry, Jill,
but you have to go.
Now that your mother
will be working,
there will be no one here
to look after you."

"I can look after myself," said Jill.
Her mother shook her head.
"No, Jill, not this summer.
You are too young
to be left alone all day."
"It's not fair!" Jill said,
and then she cried.

# Camp KeeWee

Jill watched her parents drive away.
She had a lump in her throat.

"Come on. I'll show you around,"
said Bob Burns,
who ran Camp KeeWee.
He picked up her duffle bag.
"Whew! What do you have in here?
Bricks?" he asked.
"No, books," said Jill.

"Good," said Bob Burns.
"You'll have fun trading books
with your new friends."
Jill said nothing.
She would not have fun.
She would not make friends.
She would hate the food.
And she would be the only camper
who could not go to sleep
without her teddy bear.

A big dog ran up to Jill.
He wagged his tail
and jumped on her.
"Down, Shaggy, down!"
said Bob Burns.
But Shaggy did not get down.

"He wants to play,"
said Bob Burns.
He picked up a stone
and threw it as far as he could.
The dog ran after the stone.
"Let's go before he comes back,"
said Bob Burns.
And I'll be the only camper
who doesn't love
that slobbering big dog,
said Jill to herself.

“Here’s your cabin,”
said Bob Burns.

He put her bag down.
"Come on," he said.
"You're just in time
to go hiking with the Bunnies."

"With the what?" asked Jill.
"The Bunnies.
That's the name
of your group," he said.
Jill made a face.
They must be
a bunch of dumb bunnies
to pick a name like that,
she thought.

The Bunnies were at the flagpole.
There were tall Bunnies,
short Bunnies, fat Bunnies,
and skinny Bunnies.
All of them had on
Camp KeeWee T-shirts.

And all of them had a buddy.

"This is our new Bunny,"

Bob Burns said to the counselor.

"Hi! I'm Nancy," she said.

"You can be my buddy today."

Then all the Bunnies began hiking.

# The Bunnies Play the Bobcats

SHOWERS

The next morning
Jill woke up grouchy.
Her bed was hard
and bugs had buzzed all night.

But she perked up
when Nancy said,
"Today we play softball
with the Bobcats."
The Bunnies cheered.
"We'll beat them this time!"
they yelled.

After breakfast

they ran to the ball field.

A big Bunny ran up to Jill.

"I'm Red," she said.

"I'm the pitcher.

I'm the captain, too.

Are you good at softball?"

Jill smiled.
"I play with the boys
all the time," she said.
Red suddenly flipped
the ball to Jill.

"Catch!" she said.

Jill was not expecting it

and she fumbled the ball.

"You can play right field today,"

said Red.

Rats! thought Jill.

She doesn't think I'm any good.

Well, I'll show her!

Jill stood in right field
and waited for her chance.
But no balls came near right field.

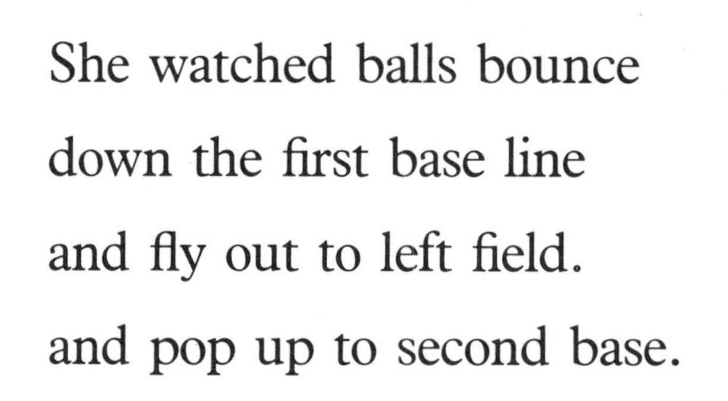

She watched balls bounce
down the first base line
and fly out to left field.
and pop up to second base.

Batting was no better.

The first time at bat

Jill hit a hard line drive.

But the Bobcat shortstop

jumped high and caught it.

The second time at bat
Jill walked.
Her last time at bat
she swung hard–
once, twice, three times.

She struck out.

And the bases were loaded.

The Bobcats

beat the Bunnies 6-5.

Jill felt terrible.

# The Rescue

That afternoon in free period
some of the girls played jacks,
others played Ping-Pong,
some went to arts and crafts.
Everyone had something to do
and someone to do it with.
Everyone but Jill.
Jill took some writing paper
and walked into the woods.

She sat under a tree
and began writing:

Dear Mom and Dad,
I hate it here.
Please take me
home.

Suddenly a flash of fur
flew by Jill.
It was a little cat.
Then a second flash of fur
flew by.
It was Shaggy.

The big dog snapped
at the little cat's tail.
And the cat ran up
the nearest tree.
Shaggy stood below,
barking and jumping.

He could almost reach the cat.
"Oh, that poor little thing,"
said Jill. "Come here, Shaggy!"

But Shaggy did not come.

He jumped higher and higher.

Then Jill had an idea.
She picked up a stone
and held it out to Shaggy.

"Go get it, boy!"
She threw the stone
as far as she could.

Shaggy ran after it.
He found the stone right away
and brought it back to Jill.

Then he rushed back to the tree.
"He found the stone
too quickly." Jill sighed.

Then she saw a big hollow tree.
The hole in the trunk
was not too high
and it was not too low.
It was just right for Jill's plan.
"Here, Shaggy, get the stone!"
She threw the stone
at the hollow tree.
Plop went the stone
right in the hole.
It was a bull's-eye!

Shaggy ran after the stone.
He scratched and sniffed
at the big hollow tree.
Then he stuck his nose
in the hole.
He could see the stone,
but he could not reach it.

He barked and jumped
and ran around the tree.
He would not leave the tree
until he got his stone.
Jill heard a low soft whistle.
It was Red.
"That was some throw!
You're a better pitcher
than I am," said Red.
"You might be just what we
need to beat the boys."

Jill grinned.

Then the two girls got the cat down from the tree.

"Wait till the kids hear
how you fooled Shaggy.
We can't stand that dog,"
said Red.
"Me, too," said Jill.
"Look, I'm Shaggy," said Red.
She let her tongue hang out
and she jumped up and down.

Jill and Red giggled.
They walked back to camp
together.

# The Secret Weapon

It was the last week of camp.
When free period came
Jill always had something to do
and someone to do it with.
But today she went off by herself.

SEE YOU LATER!
JENNY

She got out her writing paper
and wrote:

Dear Mom and Dad,
I am having a
great time! We Played
Softball today with
the boys' camp.
We won!
I was the Pitcher
and I hit a
home run.

Boy! were they
Surprised!
The girls call me
Camp Kee wee's
Secret Weapon.
Love from
Jill.
P.S. Wait till the
gang at home see
me Pitch!
XXXX
OOOO

THE END

JANET SCHULMAN was born in Pittsburgh, Pennsylvania, and was graduated from Antioch College in Yellow Springs, Ohio. She has been a copywriter, advertising manager, and marketing director for major publishers of children's books in New York City. Ms. Schulman is the author of other Greenwillow Read-alone Books, including *The Big Hello* and *Jenny and the Tennis Nut*. She and her husband and daughter Nicole live in New York City.

MARYLIN HAFNER studied at Pratt Institute and the School of Visual Arts in New York City, and in her early career did advertising illustration and fabric design. She continues to do editorial illustrations for leading magazines and has illustrated many distinguished books, including *Mind Your Manners* by Peggy Parish, *It's Halloween* by Jack Prelutsky, and *Jenny and the Tennis Nut* by Janet Schulman. Ms. Hafner has three daughters and lives in Cambridge, Massachusetts.

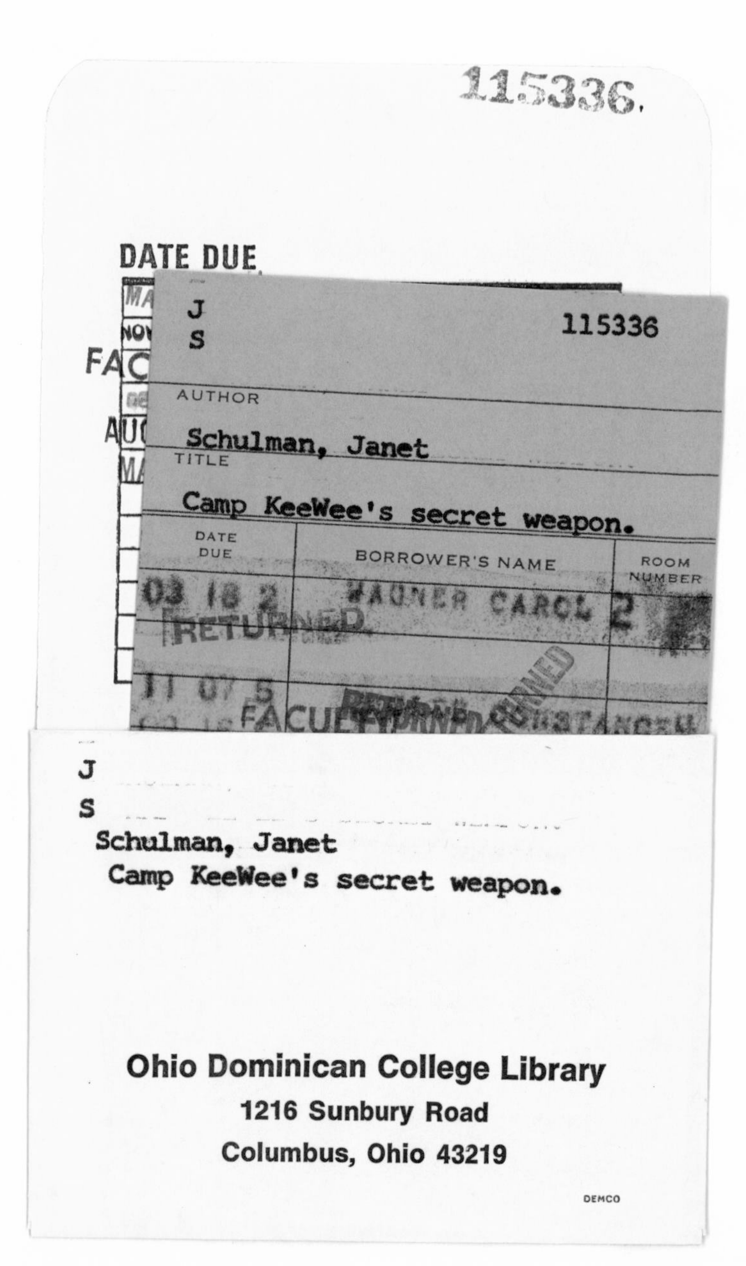
115336
DATE DUE
J
S
115336
AUTHOR
Schulman, Janet
TITLE
Camp KeeWee's secret weapon.
DATE DUE
BORROWER'S NAME
ROOM NUMBER
RETURNED
J
S
Schulman, Janet
Camp KeeWee's secret weapon.
Ohio Dominican College Library
1216 Sunbury Road
Columbus, Ohio 43219
DEMCO